KATHRYN LASKY

Sea Swan

illustrated by
CATHERINE STOCK

Macmillan Publishing Company • New York

Text copyright © 1988 by Kathryn Lasky • Illustrations copyright © 1988 by Catherine Stock
All rights reserved. No part of this book may be reproduced or transmitted in any form or by any means, electronic or
mechanical, including photocopying, recording, or by any information storage and retrieval system, without permission in writing
from the Publisher. Macmillan Publishing Company, 866 Third Avenue, New York, NY 10022. Collier Macmillan Canada, Inc.
Printed and bound in Japan

First American Edition 10 9 8 7 6 5 4 3 2 1

The text of this book is set in 16 point Perpetua.
The illustrations are rendered in colored pencil and watercolor.
Title calligraphy by Leah Palmer Preiss

Library of Congress Cataloging-in-Publication Data
Lasky, Kathryn.
Sea swan/by Kathryn Lasky; illustrated by Catherine Stock.—1st American ed.   p.   cm.
Summary: At the age of seventy-five, Elzibah Swan decides to take up swimming, a pastime which
enriches her life and one which she shares through letters with her young grandchildren.
ISBN 0-02-751700-4
[1. Old age—Fiction. 2. Grandmothers—Fiction. 3. Swimming—Fiction.]
I. Stock, Catherine, ill. II. Title.
PZ7.L3274Se 1988 [E]—dc19   88-1444 CIP AC

For Ginny Walton,
a beautiful swimmer
—K.L.

For Molly D'Arcy Thompson
—C.S.

Elzibah Swan lived on Boston's Beacon Hill in a tall brick house that her great-grandfather had built. Her grandfather, a sea captain, had brought treasures to the house all the way from China, and her own father had added a greenhouse for indoor plants. When Elzibah's husband was alive, he once brought her a beautiful tree called Falling Rain for the garden.

Elzibah had lived all her life in this house. Since her son, Nathaniel, had married and moved his family to Chicago, she had lived quietly, with only her cat, Zanzibar, and Mr. and Mrs. Fortly for company.

Mrs. Fortly cooked and cleaned. Mr. Fortly helped Elzibah in the garden and drove the car. Zanzibar played, ate, and napped. Zanzibar watched and listened, too.

"To the library," Elzibah would say each week to Zanzibar, and every Monday Fortly would drive her there. At the library she checked out books on history, gardening, and poetry.

On Tuesdays Elzibah met with her Great Books club and talked about people in books, and words, and large ideas. Wednesdays were spent at the symphony, listening to beautiful music, and Thursdays were devoted to her garden club. Each Friday she and Zanzibar rested in the sun room just between the Jerusalem cherry plant and the Amazon lily.

One Friday morning Elzibah received a letter from Chicago.

"Zanzibar!" she exclaimed. "Nathaniel's children, Claire and Jeremy, are finally coming for a visit."

It was a busy week. Elzibah and the children went to ice cream parlors and movies, played Chinese checkers until midnight, and then went out into the garden to see the deadly nightshade that only bloomed in darkness.

Although Elzibah did not know how to swim, Fortly drove them all to the beach, where the children swam and ducked and leaped over, under, and through the curling surf. They swam as Elzibah thought only a fish could.

The night before they left, Elzibah took Claire and Jeremy on a last tour of the garden. As they made wishes on night-blooming flowers and first stars, Elzibah whispered to Claire, "When you get home, please write to me." And to Jeremy she gave a packet of coral bell seeds for the garden he was planning in Chicago.

The next day Fortly drove them all to the airport. As Elzibah waved good-bye, she thought, No more Chinese checkers, but more time for reading.

Instead of reading, however, she found herself thinking constantly about Claire and Jeremy. On Thursday she wrote,

Dear Claire and Jeremy,

I was walking to the garden club meeting today, and I saw that cat. You know which one I mean, the Ambroses' cat. Such nice people to have such an awful cat! I am sure that he took Zanzibar's felt mouse. Garden club was nice. We ate chocolate cake, the kind you love, from the bakery on Charles Street. Tomorrow is my seventy-fifth birthday. I think I'll buy one of those cakes and have a piece for breakfast. You can do those kinds of things when you're seventy-five.

Love,
Grandma

Elzibah put down her pen for a moment and turned to Zanzibar. "Seventy-five!" She sighed. "My goodness, time flies!"

On the day of her seventy-fifth birthday, Elzibah Swan woke up in the big double bed that her grandfather had brought all the way from China.

She turned to Zanzibar and said, "You know, I've done lots of things in my life. I've traveled to Tibet and made an orange rose grow from a red and a yellow one. When little Nathaniel was sick with scarlet fever, I turned his bedroom into a ship's cabin, with a bunk for a bed and a hammock for reading and a window just like a porthole. But sometimes, Zanzibar, I feel..." She looked at her cat and laughed softly. "I feel helpless! More helpless than a cat!"

She laughed again. And just then she decided what she would do about it. She would learn something new. While there were many things that she couldn't do—drive a car, play chess, cook—there was only one thing she couldn't do that she wanted to do. Swim!

"Zanzibar, I am going to learn how to swim."

As soon as she had finished her breakfast, Elzibah asked Fortly to drive her to a department store. There she picked out an emerald green swimsuit with pictures of water lilies on the skirt.

Next Elzibah went to a club, where she signed up for eight swimming lessons. She began that very day.

At her first lesson she got in the water and kicked her feet like scissors.

At her second lesson she put her face in the water.

At her third lesson she practiced floating on her stomach with the teacher's help and moving her arms. That night she wrote a letter to Claire and Jeremy.

Dear Claire and Jeremy,

Guess what? I have joined a swim club and have started taking swimming lessons. I have learned how to float on my stomach and kick my feet. Thank you for the mouse for Zanzibar. We won't let this one out of sight.

Love,

Grandma

At her fourth lesson Elzibah was taught how to push off from the side and glide face down until she had to breathe. Then she practiced floating on her back.

In the fifth lesson she learned how to breathe by turning her head to the side.

In the sixth lesson she tried breathing, moving her arms, and kicking all at once. It was hard.

> *Dear Claire and Jeremy,*
>
> *I can breathe, move my arms, and kick all at the same time. Not bad for a seventy-five-year-old!*
>
> *Love and wet xxx's,*
>
> *Grandma*

By lesson seven Elzibah managed to swim four strokes, but she forgot to kick.

By lesson eight she could swim ten strokes at one time, and kick. At the end of this lesson she signed up for eight more. And she asked the lifeguard when he was on duty so that she could practice in between lessons.

Every day Elzibah swam better and swam longer distances. She began opening her eyes underwater. She saw the painted tiles of blue and green fish that decorated the pool. When she could swim the whole length of the pool several times without stopping, Elzibah began dreaming of summer and swimming in the sea.

One day Elzibah wrote to the children,

Dear Claire and Jeremy,

Yesterday Fortly drove me to a place north of Boston called Cape Ann. There is a niche in the coast where the sea furrows in to make a cove. The water is always calm, and the fish are small. The rocks are good for picnics, the sand is right for castles, and, best of all, the water is perfect for swimming.

Love,

Grandma

The land had been bought by her father, and when she was a little girl Elzibah had gone there for picnics, but she had never been allowed to go near the water. Now she was seventy-five and she could swim, and no one could tell her not to go near the water.

Every day, except when it rained, Fortly drove Elzibah to the cove with a picnic packed by Mrs. Fortly. Elzibah would swim for hours in the cool salt water. She loved to float on her back and watch the clouds move across the sky.

In the early fall evenings, back in Boston in her tall red brick house, Elzibah began drawing plans for another house, a small house made of wood, by the sea. The house was to be very simple, just one floor with one bedroom, one bathroom, one sitting room with a big window facing the cove, a kitchen with a cat door.

"Yes," she said, looking up at Zanzibar. "You deserve a cat door so you can come and go as you please. It's the country, after all, not the city. No traffic, no tomcats, no thugs." She laughed and scratched Zanzibar's neck.

Before the first frost Fortly and his two grandsons began to dig the foundation for the new house.

In early October Elzibah wrote,

Dear Claire and Jeremy,

The weather has turned cool, so guess what I bought today? A rubber wet suit so I can swim and stay warm. I do love sea swimming so much.

Love,

Grandma

She swam in her wet suit until one late afternoon in November. That afternoon she was floating on her back and watching the sun set to the west like a huge orange pumpkin drifting on dark water when snowflakes started to fall. It's time to go back to the swimming club, Elzibah thought as a snowflake landed on her nose.

That winter Elzibah took a class in water ballet. She learned how to float on her back and stick one leg up in the air.

Dear Claire and Jeremy,

Happy Valentine's Day! My new house is coming along. Guess what I've decided to call it? Sea Swan. I'm teaching myself to cook now. I can make three things: pancakes for breakfast (which Zanzibar likes better than cat food), eggs for lunch, and chowder for dinner. I think that's enough to know how to cook. There is a spot just by the house under some tall pines that will be perfect for your tents when you come to visit this August.

Love and lots of xxx's,
Grandma

As soon as the weather turned warm, Elzibah spent her days near her new house by the sea. While the workmen finished the house, she swam in the cool water of the cove, and Zanzibar watched from a rock.

Elzibah bought a face mask and tube, so she could breathe with her face in the water and watch the life on the sea bottom. She explored the rocky roots of a little island just a few feet from the shore, and she saw schools of silvery fish weaving through the tall sea grass.

She loved the sea garden, with its dappled light and water wind that slowly moved the sea grass. It was a garden that never needed to be weeded, only watched, a garden always moving and sliding with light and stirred by the liquid wind.

She planted a regular garden, too, with cucumbers and tomatoes and green beans and carrots and five different kinds of lettuce. "That is plenty to eat," she said to herself.

Finally it was time to move. One hot summer day Mr. and Mrs. Fortly drove Elzibah and Zanzibar to the new house. The car was loaded with furniture and clothing and food and books and records and a record player.

When they had finished unpacking, Elzibah invited Mr. and Mrs. Fortly for lunch. She made chowder and salad with five kinds of lettuce and an omelet.

After lunch they all put on their bathing suits. Mrs. Fortly waded and Mr. Fortly swam in circles. Zanzibar watched.

Holding Mrs. Fortly's hand, Elzibah led her into deeper water and gave her the glass mask so she could bend over and watch the sea garden.

That evening, alone for the first time in her life, Elzibah watched the sun float low in the sky. Zanzibar, full of pancakes, nestled in her lap.

She looked out of the sitting room window at the water and the sky and thought about her two gardens: the sea garden and the one with five different kinds of lettuce. She scratched Zanzibar's neck until his eyes became amber slits, and told him about the water wind and Mrs. Fortly's wonder at what she saw through the glass mask. She thought about herself, too.

"I can only cook pancakes and eggs and fish chowder," she said quietly to Zanzibar. "But I never feel hungry for anything else. It is plenty, isn't it, Zanzibar?"

Then she ran her fingers through his fur, laughed softly, and said, "But perhaps when Claire and Jeremy visit, I'll try a chocolate cake."